Peachy and Keen

SPIRIT WEEK SHOWDOWN

PEACHY and KEEN

SPIRIT WEEK SHOWDOWN

by Jason Tharp
and J. B. Rose

SCHOLASTIC INC.

Fellow Dreamer,
Continue chasing your dreams,
believing in yourself, and embracing
your "weirdness." Be brave and bold, and if the
"thing" you dream of doesn't exist, be brave
enough to stand up and make it happen.

Be the weiRd YOU want
to see in the woRld!

I believe in you,
Jason

For Dylan & Logan, my favorite dream chasers

ISBN 978-1-338-27050-1

10 9 8 7 6 5 4 3 2   18 19 20 21 22

Printed in the U.S.A.   40
First printing 2018

Book design by Suzanne LaGasa

Contents

Cats and Vlogs!

"Okay, everyone!" Peachy the cat called out in her most official voice. "Let's get this meeting started!"

No one seemed to hear her. The staff of *Purrfect9*, Happy Tails School's new online student magazine, was sitting around the table chatting loudly to each other.

"The secret is you have to use bananas that are still green," Nanner the monkey said to Rocco, *Purrfect9*'s faculty advisor, as he offered Rocco something in a bright yellow bag.

A few seats over, a cat named Rue was painting her claws dark purple and talking to a unicorn named Gertie. "You know, you should really consider horn jewelry," she said. "It's the latest trend with all rhinos on the runway this season."

"*Ahem*," Peachy cleared her throat, trying again to get everyone's attention.

"Nah, horn jewelry is a bad idea," Connie the octopus replied to Rue. "There was a goat on my field hockey team who wore it during practice once and she got it caught on—"

"NOOOOO!"

Everyone suddenly went silent and turned to look at Keen, a dog dressed in his favorite dinosaur costume. He was looking down at his phone, which was playing the familiar sounds of his favorite *Hot Diggity Dog* video game.

Keen looked up sheepishly.

"Sorry," he said. "I accidentally let the bank robber trick me into helping him escape." He shook his head and mumbled to himself, "Rookie mistake."

Peachy cut in while everyone was still quiet. "Right, so, like I was saying—time for the meeting to begin!"

Peachy and Keen were best friends, and they had started *Purrfect9* together just a few weeks ago at the beginning of the school year. Peachy was smart and super organized, and Keen was more of a fly-by-the-seat-of-your-tail kind of dog. But they had been best friends fur-ever, and that would never change. Still, as editor in chief, Peachy had to keep everyone in line—even Keen!

Peachy cleared her throat. "As you all know, our big *Purrfect9* website launch a few weeks ago was pretty successful. We've published some extra special articles that our readers really loved, like 'What to Do When You've Barked Up the Wrong Tree' by Gertie and 'How Lizards Can Love Fashion: Shedding Your Skin in Style' by Rue."

"Woo, yeah! Way to go, all you cool critters!" said Rocco, raising his hoofs in celebration.

Peachy smiled. "Rocco's right! We should all be proud of ourselves. But we haven't updated the website much in the past week. We should try to post something brand-new every day to keep our readers interested! Right now, the last thing we published was three days ago: Nanner's article about, um, the ingredients in the cafeteria's Cactus Casserole."

"It was a slow news day!" Nanner said defensively.

"Yes, maybe things have been a bit quiet around school lately," Peachy admitted. "But we just have to get creative! That's why I'd like to brainstorm new ideas to make sure *Purrfect9* stays—well, purrfect!"

"I have something," Rue said. She paused dramatically, twisting her polish bottle closed and blowing on her claws. "Tomorrow, School Spirit Week officially starts. Which means everyone in school will be wearing crazy costumes every day until the big pup rally and football game on Friday."

"Aw, yeah!" said Keen. "Already got my outfits all picked out. This pup is ready to rally!"

The magical and majestic unicorn. Notice all the magical sparkles firing off. This is the sure sign of a brilliant idea!

Mr. Fly's Science Corner

"We better *crush* the Pawcademy Pirates in that game," said Connie, slamming a curled tentacle on her desk for emphasis.

"I bet I can get some great costume pictures for my fashion column," Rue finished, ignoring the comments from the others. "And readers can even vote each day on what costumes they liked the best."

"That's a great idea, Rue," Peachy said, trying not to look too overexcited that Rue had actually just said something without being too snooty. "That's just what I'm looking for! Come on, everyone, what else?"

"I have an idea, too!" said Gertie, her skin glowing extra sparkly the way it always did when she was super excited. "What if *Purrfect9* isn't just articles and pictures? What if we have videos, too? We can start a vlog!"

"Vlog?" asked Connie, confused.

"Gesundheit," said Rocco, offering Gertie a hanky that looked like it could use a wash.

Gertie laughed. "I didn't sneeze, Rocco! Vlog is short for video blog. You know, videos about a certain topic. There's a ton of them on MooTube—but we could make our own just for *Purrfect9*. Like, instead of just writing my advice for our readers, I could talk to them on camera."

Peachy beamed. "That's an amazing idea, Gertie!" She immediately pulled her pencil from behind her ear and began scribbling notes in her notebook.

"Yeah!" Keen agreed, suddenly getting a twinkle in his eye. "But you know what would make it even BETTER?

We could play pranks around school and catch them on video! And film ourselves doing super cool action stunts—like on *Hot Diggity Dog!*"

Connie nodded. "Now we're talking! I could get some fishing line from my uncle Sal that would be perfect for a tightrope walk over the pool—"

"Ooh, yeah, and we could steal some coconuts from the cafeteria and make a catapult using stuff from the science lab—"

"Whoa, whoa, whoa," said Peachy, holding up her paws. "How did we go from a vlog about giving advice to one about crazy stunts that will probably get someone hurt?"

"No one's gonna watch videos that are all *talking*," said Keen. "No offense, Gertie. Your vlog idea is really cool—I just think we need to make it more exciting. It needs action!" Keen jumped off his chair and did a fancy kick to demonstrate, accidentally knocking Rue's claw polish all over her notes. She glared at him.

"But don't you think it's better to create videos that could help our readers?" said Gertie. "What's the point of a video about catapulting coconuts?"

Connie opened her mouth to retort, but Peachy stopped her. "Wait! I have an idea for how we can decide this. Let's have a contest!"

Connie rubbed two of her tentacles together and grinned. "I'm liking the sound of that."

"We'll break into two teams," Peachy continued. "Team Gertie and Team Keen. Each team will make a vlog channel and post videos on it throughout the week. Whichever team has the most total views at the end of the week wins, and gets to permanently host the official *Purrfect9* vlog fur-ever!"

Keen punched a fist into the air. "Yeah, Team Keen! I'm in."

"Me too," said Connie.

"Me three!" said Gertie. She shook Keen's paw. "May the best vlog win!"

Monkey Business

Don't be nutty!

At the end of the staff meeting, Connie and Keen made a beeline for Rue and tried to convince her to join their vlog team.

"You can help us beat Gertie and Peachy!" said Connie.

Rue sniffed. "Do I look like the type to enjoy making a coconut catapult?"

"Okay, that was just *one* idea . . ." said Keen.

"Well, I'm not crazy about any of the ideas," said Rue. "Including Gertie's and Peachy's. You're right about that, at least—watching those two blab away about other students' problems sounds *très* boring. But as much as I'd like to see the purrfect Peachy lose something for once, I'm not about to put *this*"—Rue pointed to her face—"in danger for a silly video stunt. Sorry." She grabbed her purse and flounced away, not looking very sorry at all.

Meanwhile, on the other side of the room, Gertie and Peachy weren't having much luck getting Nanner to join their team, either. "No can do, friends," he said. "As much as I'd love to help you win, a business monkey, such as myself, can't pass up such a perfect opportunity to promote my latest creation: Nanner Noms!"

"What are Nanner Noms?" asked Gertie.

Nanner reached into his desk drawer and whipped out a yellow bag with "Nanner Noms" printed on the front in bright orange. The o in the "Nanner Noms" logo was Nanner's face. "Nanner Noms are a new snack I made myself! I'm going to start selling them around school, and it would be *sweet* to have a commercial on your vlog channel."

"I don't know, Nanner," Peachy said doubtfully. "What's in them? We can't advertise just anything. What if they make you sick or something?"

Nanner looked offended. "They won't make you *sick*! Nanner Noms are delicious and nutritious. I'm not just monkeyin' around with this—see for yourself." He offered the bag to Peachy. She took a small handful of the little brown cookies shaped like Nanner's grinning face and suspiciously bit into one.

"Oooh! Okay, that's pretty good," she admitted, talking with her mouth full. "What's in them?"

"A complicated and top secret recipe . . . I may or may not have had help from my dad," Nanner said. "So whad'ya think about advertising on your channel? I'll give you each a free bag of Nanner Noms if you let me."

"Make it five bags!" said Peachy as she eagerly reached for another handful. Gertie giggled.

"Five each?! That's almost my entire first batch! My dad—uh, I mean, I'll have to do a lot of baking to restock." Nanner thought it over. "How about three?" he suggested.

Peachy smiled and popped another cookie into her mouth. "Deal!"

After Nanner had convinced Keen and Connie to advertise Nanner Noms on their channel, too, he headed to his locker in a great mood. He was whistling down the hallway when he passed by Rue at her locker and got an idea.

"Hey, Rue," he said. "How would you like to be on camera in front of the whole school?"

Rue rolled her eyes. "I already told Keen and Connie that I don't want to be in their crazy videos."

"No, not that," said Nanner. "I'm not in the contest, either. I'm using both of the channels to advertise a snack I made called Nanner Noms. And I could use a fashionable sidekick like you to help me sell it!"

Rue's eyes flashed. "Excuse me, what? You want me to be a *sidekick*?" she hissed.

Nanner backed away a couple of steps. "What? Uh, no, no, no, sorry. Not sidekick. I meant, uh, stylist! You can be my stylist for the ads. You know, make sure everything looks good." He straightened his bow tie. "Like you said, Spirit Week starts tomorrow. I want to make sure my costumes look super fresh on camera."

Rue closed her locker and broke into a rare smile. "Now you're talking my language, banana brain."

Let the Games Begin

The next day, Keen was wearing a brown vest, tie-dyed headband, and round peace-sign sunglasses—which actually wasn't very out of the ordinary. Connie was wearing a flower crown headband and a peace sign necklace, which was definitely out of the ordinary. That could only mean one thing—it was the start of Happy Tails School Spirit Week, with Happenin' Hippie Day!

It was just before lunch and Team Keen was in the *Purrfect9* staff room, getting ready to film their first video. Keen had come up with the purrfect idea for their first stunt while watching *Hot Diggity Dog* the night before, and he was explaining it to Connie.

". . . So then the police think he's the bad guy," Keen said, breathless from acting out some of the scenes as he spoke. "It's all a big mistake, but every time Hot

Diggity Dog tries to explain, they just chase him anyway. And he ends up running toward the end of the mountain! There's nowhere else to go! It's a pretty steep drop below, so he looks around and grabs a giant leaf from a plant in the forest and uses it to surf down the hill to safety!"

Connie's mouth dropped open in an O shape as she realized where Keen's idea was going. "So for our video, are you thinking—"

"We're gonna surf down Hedgehog Hill! And hopefully get enough air to fly over the pond at the bottom."

Hedgehog Hill was right behind Happy Tails School. It got its name from the group of older hedgehog students who liked to roll down it after school—and the hill was very, very steep. Most other animals didn't dare try to play on it.

Connie never shied away from taking a risk. "That's an awesome idea! Let's do it!" she said.

"All right!" said Keen, happy that his teammate was on board. "We just need to figure out what we can use to surf. I don't think we'll be able to get away with giant leaves in this case."

"Yeah, that stuff only works in cartoons." Connie tapped her head with a tentacle thoughtfully. "What about cafeteria trays? We just have to sneak two away during lunch when Mrs. Belle isn't looking."

Keen bounced excitedly. "Yeah! That'll work! Watch out Hot Diggity Dog, Octopup is coming for you!"

That same morning, Peachy and Gertie sent out a *Purrfect9* news blast straight to their readers' PinePhones:

To: Happy Tails Student Body
Subject: Be Pawsitive

Listen up, Happy Tails!
Are you dealing with a ruff problem? Need some advice for how to handle a hairy situation? What better way than to watch Be Pawsitive!, Peachy and Gertie's new advice and lifestyle vlog on Purrfect9. Reply to this email address with your questions, and then check out Be Pawsitive! later today to hear what tips and tricks we may have for you!

"Are you sure this is going to work?" Gertie had asked when Peachy clicked SEND. "I get some emails with questions for my regular advice column on the website, but those come in slowly over days or a whole week! How are we going to get enough questions for our first video in just a couple of hours?"

"Don't worry," Peachy answered confidently. "There's always a Happy Tails student in need!"

But a couple of hours came and went, and by late afternoon, no one had responded to Peachy and Gertie's call for questions. They were back in the staffroom during the last period of the day, which Gertie and Peachy both had free for study hall. Peachy had begun anxiously snacking on her stash of Nanner Noms, getting crumbs all over the flowy flowered dress she was wearing for Happenin' Hippie Day.

"Why doesn't anyone in this school have any problems?!" Peachy shouted in frustration.

Gertie raised an eyebrow.

"Uh, I mean, I don't *want* anyone to have problems,"

Peachy explained quickly. "You know what I mean! I just want to help someone with our vlog."

"I know," Gertie agreed. "Me too. I think we just need to give it more ti—"

DING!

Gertie froze. That sound was coming from her

PinePhone—it was telling her that someone had emailed with a question! She and Peachy pounced on her phone to read the message. Gertie cleared her throat and read it out loud:

"'Dear Gertie and Peachy, I am writing with a very

serious question. What can you do to make sure you are a gracious loser? Like when you two see that Connie and Keen's vlog is super awesome and hilarious and is going to beat you in the contest? Are you ready for that??? YOU SHOULD BE! HAHAHA! Sincerely, Octopup.'"

Gertie paused. "Something tells me this is not a real reader question."

28

Peachy narrowed her eyes. "'Octopup?' Ugh. It's Connie and Keen! They're just trying to mess with us and throw us off our game. Forget about the emails, Gertie. I have an idea. We're going to make a great vlog no matter what!"

Vlogs Away!

Connie and Keen were at the very top of Hedgehog Hill, cafeteria trays in hand. It was trickier than they thought to sneak the trays away from the cafeteria cow, Mrs. Belle, after lunch. Mrs. Belle had spotted them trying to casually stroll out of the cafeteria with their trays behind their backs, and shouted across the room to stop them.

"Hey, you two! Where do you think you're going with my trays? You know those can't leave the cafeteria."

"Uh . . . uh . . . uhmm—" Connie stuttered, trying to come up with a good excuse. Her mind was blank.

Luckily, she didn't have to say anything. A group of third-year chimps began flinging food at each other and

Mrs. Belle got distracted.

"Not AGAIN! What have I told you three about dirtying my cafeteria?!" Mrs. Belle shouted at them while Connie and Keen slipped away.

Now they were at the top of the hill with the camera set up at the bottom.

"Ready, Connie?" asked Keen, wagging his tail excitedly.

Connie gulped. This hill was much higher than she remembered. "Are you . . . sure this is a good idea, Keen? What if we don't make it over the pond?"

"It's gonna be fine! And hey, even if we mess up and land right in the water, it'll be hilarious. Remember that MooTube video of the polar bear that kept slipping on ice? Everyone loves watching crazy wipeouts and all that stuff!"

▶ ▶| 🔊 0:00 / 4:23

"Yeah, that's true . . ." Connie admitted. *Crazy wipeouts?* She was still a little nervous, but no way was she backing out now. "Okay, well, here goes nothing!"

Connie and Keen got on their trays, gave the camera a little salute, and pushed themselves over the edge of the hill.

"AHHHHHHH!" Connie yelled.

"COWABUNGAAAAAA!" screamed Keen.

"Hello, everyone, and happy Happenin' Hippie Day!" Peachy announced, smiling at the camera. "Welcome to *Be Pawsitive!* On this very special *Purrfect9* vlog, Gertie here and I will answer questions straight from all of YOU and share our best advice. Take it away with our first question, Gertie."

"Well, Peachy, this one is a horn-scratcher. But I think we can help!" Gertie answered, hoping that her sparkles didn't cause a bad glare on camera. "This student wrote: 'Dear Gertie and Peachy, I have a little sister who copies EVERYTHING that I say and do! I know this is a phase that all parrots go through when they're first born, even me—but I grew out of it when I was two. My sister is five and still copies me all the time! It's driving me crazy. What do I do to get her to stop? Sincerely, Peeved Parrot.'"

"That is a tough one, Gertie," Peachy said seriously, pretending that she had not just written that question herself ten minutes ago. She and Gertie had decided to write a question and just act as if someone had sent it in—who would know the difference? Peachy had come up with this question after remembering a problem her friend Polly had with her little brother. So, it wasn't *really* a lie, right? "What would you suggest?"

"Well, Peeved Parrot," Gertie replied, speaking into the camera. "Being copied all the time must get very annoying. But I suspect that, in this case, it is not only your family's parrot ancestry that is the cause. I think she truly wishes she was just like you! She probably thinks her older sibling is super cool and just wants to follow in your flight patterns. Maybe try inviting her to some fun things with your friends once in a while, so she feels included! Then she won't have to copy you to feel like she's part of your cool world."

"Very wise words, Gertie!" Peachy said. "Good luck, Peeved Parrot! And now, here's a word from our sponsor, Nanner Noms!"

Nanner and Rue entered from off camera. They had taken Happenin' Hippie Day to the next level. Rue had a flowery scarf tied around her head like a bandanna and a big fancy shawl with tassels draped over her shoulders. Nanner was wearing a long dark wig, fake moustache, and bell-bottom pants. They had the best Spirit Week costumes that Peachy and Gertie had seen all day!

FAR OUT, MAN!

"Hello there, all my Happy Tails Hippies!" said Nanner. "I'm sure you're all having a groovy day, but you know what would make it even GROOVIER? Nanner Noms, that's what!" He pulled out the bright yellow bag and held it up to the camera. "No more boring, flavorless snacks . . ." He suddenly looked meaningfully at Rue, waiting for her to say her line.

Rue rolled her eyes but held up a carrot and took a small bite. "Blah. This doesn't taste good at all," she said in a flat voice, clearly not trying very hard.

Nanner continued with enough enthusiasm for the both of them. "Of course it doesn't! Because it's not Nanner Noms, the most far-out, sweetest snack ever invented! Just one *piece*"—Nanner made a hippie peace sign with his hands and winked—"and you'll be hooked. And at only five dollars a bag, what a bargain! Stop by locker four hundred eighty-three to buy Nanner Noms before they're all gone!"

"And, cut!" said Gertie, switching off the camera. "Great job, everyone!" She brought her phone to a nearby computer and began to upload the video to the *Purrfect9* website.

"And now, we wait," said Peachy, reaching into the open bag of Nanner Noms.

"Hey! I gave you your own bag, you know," said Nanner. "Three, actually."

Peachy decided not to confess that she had only one bag left.

Nanner and Rue left, but Peachy and Gertie hung around the staffroom for the rest of their free period. They stayed there into the after-school period, too, trying not to obsessively refresh their video page to see how many views they were getting. Finally, when they heard the last bell of the day, they both rushed over to a computer to check the video.

"Thirty-two views!" Gertie said with a smile. "I think that sounds pretty good for a video that's only been up for about an hour. We're off to a good start!"

Peachy wasn't ready to celebrate just yet. "Now let's go see how many views Connie and Keen have! I'm sure their first video is up by now, too."

Sure enough, Connie and Keen's video had been posted on their section of the *Purrfect9* vlog. Above the video was a large graphic showing Connie's and Keen's grinning faces with the words "Octopup Adventures!" flashing brightly.

Right below the video, the viewer count said—

"Ninety-five?!" Peachy shouted. "They have ninety-five views already? How? That's almost three times as many as we have!"

Gertie had clicked PLAY and was watching Connie and Keen zoom down Hedgehog Hill on cafeteria trays, then soar over the pond at the bottom, and celebrate joyfully when they landed. Gertie chuckled. "Wow, that's pretty impressive." Then she saw the look on Peachy's face. "Um, I mean, it's not *that* great. I bet anyone could do that, really . . ."

"All right, Gertie, this is going to be a tougher fight than we thought," Peachy said. "But it's only the beginning! Starting tomorrow, we're going to take our vlog to the next level. No one at Happy Tails will be able to ignore us anymore!"

A Wacky Wednesday

> **Attention,**
> ## all Happy Tails Students!
>
> Don't forget to come to class prepared for
> ## WACKY HAIR WEDNESDAY,
> the one day of the year when the worst
> hair don'ts become the best hair-DOs!
>
> And for our many students who are more
> slippery and scaly than hairy, please join in the
> school spirit as well with
> ## WACKY HAT WEDNESDAY!
>
> Whatever you wear, just make it **WACKY!**

" Microphone?"

"Check."

"Camera?"

"Check."

"Nanner Noms?"

"Che—wait, what? Why do we need Nanner Noms for this?" Gertie asked.

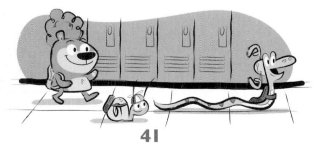

"You never know!" said Peachy, grabbing the remains of her last bag from Nanner and shoving it in the bag she and Gertie were packing.

They were preparing to take *Be Pawsitive!* on the road—well, to the school hallways. After their disappointing viewer count from yesterday's video, Peachy and Gertie decided to try a new approach for their vlog. If the Happy Tails students wouldn't come to them, they would go straight to the Happy Tails students!

"We have twenty minutes before the bell rings for homeroom," said Gertie. "Let's do this!"

Gertie and Peachy lugged their equipment bag through the halls, looking for students they could convince to talk on camera. It was even more chaotic than usual because of all the wacky hats and hair for Spirit Week. Peachy saw two deer lock antlers by accident when the glowing string lights in one pair of antlers got caught in the frilly bow of the other antlers.

Peachy decided they might as well just call out to everyone nearby at once. "Ahem—um—hi!" She waved her arms to draw attention. "Would anyone like to ask Gertie and me a question for *Be Pawsitive!?* You'll be on camera! For our vlog!"

"Anyone?" Gertie joined in. "You can ask us anything! About friends, about school . . ."

"I have one!" said a voice. Peachy and Gertie turned and saw Sheila, a koala they both knew from their math class. She sat in the last row and was often scolded by their teacher for sleeping during the lesson.

Gertie got the camera on her phone ready while Peachy held out the microphone to Sheila. "Please, go ahead!" she said encouragingly.

"Well, I'm wondering why Happy Tails doesn't have a better program for its nocturnal students," said Sheila. "It's in our nature to sleep all day, so how are we supposed to pay attention in a daytime class?"

Before Peachy could respond, another voice joined in. "You basically sleep *all* the time, Sheila, not just during the day," said a small bat Peachy didn't know. The bat looked at the camera. "But Sheila makes an important point. I'm Kitti, president of NAA, the Nighttime Animal Alliance, here at Happy Tails. We nocturnal animals face many challenges at this school. We have to stick together!"

"So, what exactly would you say is your biggest challenge, Kitti?" Peachy asked.

"It's like Sheila said. We're most active during nighttime, so that's when we do all our best thinking! But we're still expected to attend day classes like all the rest of you daytime animals. It's not fair!"

"I have to sneak in naps during lunch and study hall," added an owl who was standing nearby. A small crowd of curious students had begun to form around Peachy's interview.

"It sounds like maybe Happy Tails should offer night classes," said Peachy.

"Or *at least* special areas in the school for nocturnal animals to sleep during the day when they have a free period," added Gertie from behind the camera.

"Yes!" said Kitti enthusiastically, while other students around her nodded in agreement.

"Maybe the NAA can start a petition! What are some other problems you're all dealing with?" Peachy asked. She was so excited that they were finally having a real, important discussion for their vlog!

"Uh, there's an elephant in the room,' Kitti whispered.

Don't give up on your daydream!

Peachy raised her eyebrows. "And what would that be?"

"No, I'm trying to tell you Principal Trunx is behind you," Kitti said. "And he doesn't look happy."

Uh-oh, Peachy thought, slowly turning around to face the principal of Happy Tails. *Just what we need.* Principal Trunx had disliked Peachy from the moment he met her, on her first day at Happy Tails. He had gone to Happy Tails with her aunt Priscilla many years ago and was jealous when Priscilla became the star reporter of the old school newspaper they both wrote for, the *Happy Tails Times.* Even though it was all a very long time ago, Principal Trunx clearly had not forgotten any of it. Ever since Peachy and Keen had started *Purrfect9*, Principal

Trunx was always looking for a reason to shut it down.

As Principal Trunx got closer, the crowd scattered. No one wanted to get pulled into whatever trouble Peachy and Gertie might get into.

"What's going on here?" he asked with a scowl, looking at Gertie, who was still holding up her phone to record. "Put that device away at once!"

"Hi, Principal Trunx," said Peachy in her most polite voice. "Gertie and I were just making a v deo for *Purrfect9*. We're starting a vlog to help students."

"Is that so? Because it sounds like you were recording a video to make Happy Tails School look bad," said Principal Trunx.

"No, not at all!" said Gertie nervously. "We were just talking to students about some ways the school could get better."

"That's not for you to decide," said Principal Trunx. "And I cannot allow you to share that—vlurg—vog—er, that *video* online for all the parents to see! Delete it now."

"But—" Peachy protested.

"*Now*," Principal Trunx demanded, crossing his huge arms.

Gertie reluctantly held out her phone so Principal Trunx could watch as she deleted the video of Sheila and Kitti.

"I better not see anything like this again," he said. "After all, aren't you supposed to be showing your school spirit this week?" An odd thing for him to say, since Principal Trunx had not worn a wacky hat or styled a wacky hairstyle that day. Even though he was bald, Peachy secretly thought he had missed an opportunity to have a great wacky moustache. He clearly didn't actually care about school spirit, but Peachy knew better than to point that out.

MR. Party Pooper

KEEN

After Principal Trunx left, Peachy and Gertie gloomily walked off to their lockers before homeroom began, no closer to having a great new video to bring their vlog channel back in the running.

The Not-So-Sneaky Splash

While Gertie and Peachy were filming in the halls, Keen and Connie were in the middle of preparing for their second video, too: a hilarious prank on Principal Trunx!

They had arrived at school early and waited in the hall until Principal Trunx left his office. Then they *super quietly* snuck by the school secretary, Mrs. Marbles, while she was playing Acorn Crush on her computer. The "super quietly" part was extra hard, considering they were dragging a basket full of water balloons along with them.

BANG. Keen had accidentally knocked the basket into one of the chairs placed in the waiting area right outside Principal Trunx's office. He and Connie froze, waiting for Mrs. Marbles to turn around and catch them in the act.

Bloop. Crunch. Luckily, it seemed like the sound effects from Acorn Crush had masked their own noise. They scurried the rest of the way into the office and silently closed the door before she would notice them.

"Success!" Keen cheered, while still keeping his voice down. "Okay, let's do this before he gets back."

Keen and Connie got to work maneuvering the basket of water balloons on the very top of the bookshelf right next to Principal Trunx's door. Connie tied a string from the basket handle to the door handle. When Principal Trunx comes through the door, he'll pull on the string, bringing the water balloons down right on top of him! Connie and Keen would film the big moment from the bushes right outside his office window. No way they wouldn't win the video contest after that!

They both tried to keep their giggling quiet as they finished setting up. Suddenly, they heard Principal Trunx's booming voice outside, talking to Mrs. Marbles.

"It was that nuisance Peachy again. She's always up to something, isn't she? And our unicorn student was with her—how disappointing. I thought unicorns were supposed to have impeccable manners."

You look fantastic . . . Would you like a cookie?

Thank you. Unicorns are so nice!

"Mmm," Mrs. Marbles responded, clearly still focusing on her Acorn Crush game.

"Not even homeroom yet and students are already acting up! I tell you, the very next students I see with one paw, wing, or fin out of line will be in very serious trouble."

Inside the office, Connie and Keen exchanged worried looks. "Well, he didn't say tentacle," Connie joked, holding hers up.

"Ahh, Connie, this was a bad idea!" Keen panicked. "He's going to catch us and we'll be in so much trouble."

"We can't get detention!" Connie agreed. "Then we won't have time to make another video and we'll lose the contest!"

"Okay, let's just take this down before he comes in here and we'll think of something else," Keen said, pointing to the basket. But they heard Principal Trunx's voice getting closer and closer. He would open the door any second—so Keen did the only thing he could think of.

SPLASH!

Keen had opened the door himself and darted
through it, letting the water balloons come crashing
down on his head. Behind him, Connie rushed to pick
up the broken balloon pieces and then threw the basket
on top of her head in the nick of time. Seconds later,
Principal Trunx stood before them.

At first, the principal looked completely surprised as
he stared at the scene before him: Keen soaking wet,
his Wacky Hair Day style now sopping and ruined, and
Connie, wearing a basket that was concealing the
broken water balloon pieces underneath.

"Oh, hello, sir," said Connie, trying to act casual.

"Why do you have a basket on your head, young
lady?" he asked, still looking utterly confused.

"It's Wacky Hat Day, sir!" she answered, touching the

edge of the basket and tipping her head as far as she dared, hoping the balloon pieces wouldn't come tumbling out.

"And why are you all wet?" Principal Trunx asked Keen. "What are you two doing in front of my office?" His surprise was slowly wearing off and now he began to narrow his eyes at them suspiciously.

Keen thought fast. "It was the pipes! In the bathroom on the second floor. One of the pipes in the sink burst while I was in there and it's flooding everything! I came straight here to tell you."

Now Principal Trunx looked less suspicious and more his usual annoyed self. "Not again! Fine. I will be sure to notify Rocco and ask him to fix it."

"You know what, that's okay," Connie babbled quickly.

"We're actually about to see Rocco right now, anyway! So we'll tell him. No worries. No need to tell him. Or check on it yourself. Everything's fine!"

And with that, Connie and Keen darted out of the office, leaving a very confused principal behind them.

Right before homeroom, Peachy, Gertie, Connie, and Keen all crossed paths in the hallway. Peachy and Gertie were still disappointed that their last video had been deleted—but as soon as they saw Connie and Keen coming their way, they put on huge grins as if everything was going great.

"Hey, guys!" Peachy said a little too cheerily. "How's the filming going? Keen . . . you look a little, um, wet."

Keen shook out his fur, spraying some innocent students standing nearby. "All part of the plan, Peachy!" he lied. "Just wait till you see our next video, and you'll understand."

"What about you two?" Connie asked. "Giving lots of advice?"

"Oh, sure," said Gertie with a big grin that was not very convincing, since her skin didn't have its usual glow and sparkle.

"Hey," said Connie, looking behind them at a poster on the wall. It was advertising the big pup rally at the end of Spirit Week on Friday. "What do you say we make our contest a little more interesting?"

"What do you have in mind?" asked Peachy.

Connie pointed to the poster. "The winning team not only gets to host the *Purrfect9* vlog permanently, but also gets to film a special *live* video at the pup rally on Friday to celebrate. In front of the whole school!"

Peachy and Gertie exchanged looks. Filming at the pep rally would be pretty cool. But so far, they could barely make a good video with a few other students—did they even *want* to film something in front of the entire school?

"Of course, if you're too *chicken* . . ." Connie said in a singsong voice.

"Hey!" They all turned to see a chicken named Cooper standing nearby at his locker, frowning. "That's just rude," he said.

"Whoops, sorry, Cooper," Connie said sheepishly.

"Okay, Connie," Peachy said. "You're on! Winners are the permanent hosts *and* they'll film a video live at the pep rally. One more day to get as many views as possible!"

The teams shook on it and each went their separate ways as the bell rang for homeroom.

Teaching a Rad Dog New Tricks

FLEX YOUR FEATHERS!

After their last attempt had totally failed, Keen and Connie decided that maybe they should stay away from pulling pranks for now and go back to what had made their first video so popular: a super cool, heart pounding, fur-raising stunt! They worked on tons of ideas Wednesday during lunch, and then after school, too. Finally, the next morning, they were ready for their most ambitious video yet.

"Okay, let's go over this one more time," Connie said, looking very official while holding a clipboard and pen. On the clipboard was a diagram she and Keen had drawn of the obstacle course they set up in the gymnasium. Rocco had unlocked the gym doors for them so they could get in before the Early Bird

Weightlifting Club took over.

"So, you'll start by rolling down this ramp on the skateboard, then jump up through the Hula-Hoop and catch the Frisbee in your mouth while you're still in the air. Then land on the trampoline and end with a blackflip." Connie paused. "Sounds simple enough," she joked.

"Yeah!" said Keen, not picking up on her sarcasm. "And remember, we're gonna film it in slow motion when I catch the Frisbee going through the hoop. It's gonna be EPIC!"

"Even more epic with that outfit," Connie said with a laugh. Both she and Keen were wearing long white sheets tied on one side for that day's Spirit Week celebration, Toga Thursday.

"Let's do it!" Keen said, grabbing the skateboard and getting into position. Connie took her place with the camera and Frisbee at the other end of the gym.

ramp of
gym mats

Start

EPIC
GYM JUMP

catch Frisbee
in mouth

"Ready?" she called. Keen waved to show that he was. "Ready, set, annnd, action!"

Keen jumped on the skateboard and rolled down the ramp he and Connie had created with some gym mats. Then, at the very bottom, his long toga got snagged in one of the wheels. Keen tripped and was sent lurching forward toward the Hula-Hoop. Before Connie realized what was happening, she threw the Frisbee to Keen—but instead of catching it in his mouth, it hit him right in the nose. He got stuck in the middle of the Hula-Hoop and hung there, his tangled toga preventing him from moving.

All animals must learn to adapt, and Keen just learned the hard way.

Mr. Fly's Science Corner

NOTE TO SELF
Toga + Awesome stunts= Bad idea!

Connie rushed toward Keen to make sure he was okay. "Whoops, sorry, Keen!" she shouted. "I didn't mean to hit you!"

Luckily, once she got up close, she saw Keen was fine. He was laughing while rubbing his sore nose.

"It's okay," he said. "I guess maybe I *shouldn't* do this in the toga."

Now that she knew he wasn't hurt, Connie started laughing, too. "You look ridiculous. You should have seen your face when you were flying through the air!" Then she remembered that he *could* see it. "Hold on!" She grabbed the camera and held it up to Keen so he could watch. It was even funnier on camera because Connie had filmed it with the slow motion effect on. Keen and Connie watched it a second time and laughed even harder.

"Okay, okay, now let's try this again," said Keen, detangling himself from his toga.

"Wait a minute," Connie said, still staring at the video on her phone. "Why don't we just use this one for the vlog?"

"Use that one? No way!" said Keen. "You said it yourself, I look ridiculous. I don't want everyone in school watching that."

"Yeah, but *you* said it *yourself*," Connie pointed out. "When we surfed down Hedgehog Hill. Remember? You said everyone loves watching videos of wipeouts and bloopers, like on MooTube, because they're hilarious."

"Well . . . I don't know." Keen hesitated. "I'd rather just get the trick right."

"The version of you messing up will get way more views, and you know it," Connie said. "C'mon! This is exactly what will help us beat Peachy and Gertie and win the contest!"

Keen looked at Connie's excited face and thought it over. It was hard to argue with his own point. "Okay," he agreed. "Why not?"

Feeling Foolish

The next day at school was the final day of Spirit Week: Mismatch Day! Everyone came to class dressed in their craziest, most horribly nonmatching outfits. But even more important, it was also the last day of the vlog contest. Both teams had up until the last bell rang to get as many views as possible. Then the winner would celebrate with a video at the pup rally that night!

Keen was in reading class, trying to pay attention to Mr. Hopper and the lesson on that week's book, *The Lion, the Witch, and the Warthog.* He kept getting distracted by a small group of students sitting to his left, giggling. They all had their phones hidden behind their desks, and every time Mr. Hopper turned his back to the class for just a moment, they would nudge each other and point to something on their screens. Keen noticed them sneaking glances back at him, too.

Finally, Gisella the peacock held her phone screen out so Keen could see what they were all watching: the latest *Octopup Adventures* video, with Keen getting smacked in the nose with a Frisbee in slow motion. Gisella hit PLAY again and the group dissolved into laughter.

"Eyes up here!" Mr. Hopper ordered, finally noticing that he didn't have his class's full attention. Gisella and the others quickly hid their phones, but kept glancing at Keen and laughing.

Keen tried to laugh along, but it didn't feel right. He didn't know what his problem was. After all, Connie was right—their classmates clearly loved that video and were watching it again and again, meaning their viewer count must be getting super high! So why was he feeling like he had just watched another dog get the very last Maple-Bacon Bash at Nibbles 'n' Bits?

Because they're still laughing at me, Keen thought, *no matter how much it will help us in the contest.* It was not a nice feeling having people laugh at you, even when you pretended you were in on the joke.

Keen told himself that when this class ended, he would go to the next one and forget all about it—but that was far from the truth. His video was everywhere: in all of his classes, in the halls, during lunch. All day he heard and saw students watching it and laughing. Some saw Keen coming down the hall and made crazy faces in slow motion, like they were re-creating the video. A few students stopped Keen to tell him how many times they had watched it, as if he was as famous as *Hot Diggity Dog*. But the difference was that *Hot Diggity Dog* was famous for being awesome and catching bad guys! Now Keen was famous at Happy Tails, all right—for being a total doggy disaster.

"Three hundred seventy views?!" Peachy shouted, staring at the screen with her mouth hanging open. "Gertie, look. Connie and Keen's newest video has three hundred seventy views, and counting!"

Gertie twirled her mane worriedly. "How are we ever going to beat that by the end of the day today? We're doomed!"

Gertie and Peachy were spending their lunch break filming one last video in the *Purrfect9* staff room. Since they didn't want to get in trouble with Principal Trunx, they were sticking to answering questions that were emailed to them. Luckily, they at least had a few real questions to answer this time.

"We're not doomed!" said Peachy with a determined look on her face. "We're going to stream our last video live online so we can get as many views as possible. We still have time to stay in the game!"

"You're right," Gertie said, nodding. Her sparkles brightened as she made herself focus. "And you know what? Even if we don't win, we can still at least help whoever sent in these questions. And that's what our vlog is all about, right?"

"Right!" Peachy agreed. "Let's do this!"

They switched on the camera and set the video to stream live on *Purrfect9*. All Happy Tails students would get a notification on their phones to tune in now to the next *Be Pawsitive!* video. Gertie looked down at the emails on her phone to find the next question.

"Hello, Happy Tails, and welcome to another episode of *Be Pawsitive!* Our first question today comes from Grumbling Groundhog. Grumbling writes, 'My dad is always talking to me about following in his footsteps one day as a weatherhog, but I'm not interested. I don't want to disappoint him, but he needs to know I'm just not as passionate about predicting the weather as he is. What do I do?'"

Gertie looked into the camera as she continued. "Grumbling, I think you just need to be honest! Your dad might not even realize the pressure he's putting on you. He's just excited to share something he loves! But if you tell him how you feel, I'm sure he won't be disappointed. He just wants you to be happy."

"I agree, Gertie," said Peachy. "Good luck, Grumbling Groundhog! On to our next question . . ." Peachy scanned the screen for the next email. This one had come in just an hour ago. "This one is from Downward Doggy. It says: 'I let my friend talk me into posting a video of me looking really silly. We thought it would be funny, but now that everyone in school is

actually laughing at it, I just feel really embarrassed . . .'"
Peachy paused. She had a good feeling she knew who
this email was from. "'I guess I didn't think about how
many people would see it, and how they can watch it
over and over or share it with anyone they want. I feel
like I can never show my face in class again! Help!'"

Peachy and Gertie exchanged looks. They were
both thinking the same thing: This email was obviously
from Keen. Apparently, he wasn't very happy about the
latest *Octopup Adventures* video having 370 views, either.

"You know what, Downward Doggy?" said Peachy. "I know it might not feel like it right now, but this will all blow over in a little while. *Everyone* has embarrassing moments. And we all feel like that embarrassing moment is the end of the world! I actually had my own embarrassing moment yesterday . . . As regular viewers will know, we have advertised a snack called Nanner Noms on our vlog. I've become a bit of a fan of Nanner Noms—"

Gertie snorted and tried to disguise it as a cough.

"Okay, a *really big* fan of Nanner Noms," Peachy admitted. "I can't help it, they're so addictive! Anyway, yesterday my, um, love for Nanner Noms got a little out of control. Because my last bag was all gone, and Nanner couldn't sell me anymore right away—he has a waitlist for new orders now! Then later, I was at my locker and someone bumped into me, making my bag fall off my shoulder. And I saw some Nanner Noms crumbs spill out of my bag all over the floor, and . . . well . . ." Peachy trailed off.

"Nooooo, Peachy!" Gertie groaned, guessing what was coming next and covering her face with her hooves.

"I was craving Nanner Noms so bad, I just had to have some! Before I knew what was happening, I got down on all four paws and started eating the crumbs right off the floor!" Peachy cringed. "And guess who was standing right behind me, watching the whole thing?"

"Who?" asked Gertie in a hushed voice, fully engrossed in the story.

"Principal Trunx!" Peachy announced, and both she and Gertie erupted into laughter. "It was horrible! I was so embarrassed! But, Downward Doggy, to get back to my point—see this? That was a very embarrassing moment for me, but now it's a funny story that I can laugh about with my friend. And soon, your embarrassing feeling will turn into that, too."

Suddenly, Gertie's phone started buzzing. She looked down and saw three new emails for *Purrfect9*. She scanned them quickly and realized they were from students who were watching the vlog right now. They had sent in stories about their own embarrassing moments to help make Downward Doggy feel better! She and Peachy began reading some stories live on air, which prompted even more viewers to write in! From a dog who had been caught drinking from a toilet bowl in the restroom to a squid who had left a trail of ink on his chair in class, there were plenty of Happy Tails students willing to share their super-embarrassing stories.

Peachy and Gertie couldn't believe it. When they finally ended their video, they looked at each other with huge grins. They were definitely getting a lot of views with this video—maybe even enough to bring them back in the running for the contest! But even more important, their vlog was finally doing what they had always hoped for: offering help to the students of Happy Tails.

A Hap-*pie* Ending

"All right, cool cats and purrfect pals! Gather 'round." Rocco called to the *Purrfect9* staff in their newsroom. It was time to announce the results for the vlog contest. The pep rally would begin in only ten minutes, meaning the winning team had to be ready to film their live video in front of the school right away.

As the group made their way over to Rocco, Keen pulled Peachy and Gertie aside.

"Hey, guys," he whispered. "I just wanted to say thanks, for earlier. You probably didn't know, but I sent you that question about the video. I'm 'Downward Doggy.'"

Peachy and Gertie pretended to be shocked. "What! I had absolutely no idea," Gertie said, a little too loudly.

"Wow, me, either," said Peachy. "So . . . did our video help you, then?"

"Oh yeah, it really did!" Keen said. "I was laughing so much at all of those other stories that I forgot about what was bothering me for a minute. And then, even when I remembered . . . it was easier to laugh at myself, too." Keen looked down at his feet, a bit sheepishly. "So, I wanted to say that, and . . . Gertie, your vlog idea turned out to be a really good one."

"Thanks, Keen!" said Gertie, sparkling warmly.

They didn't realize until she spoke up that Connie had been standing nearby listening the whole time. "I wanted to say thanks, too," she said. "I felt bad that I was the one who convinced Keen to post the video when he didn't want to at first. But I'm glad your video helped him feel better." She turned to Keen. "Sorry I was so pushy, Keen."

Keen waved a paw and was about to tell Connie not to be sorry at all when they were interrupted.

"Enough yapping!" Nanner called from over by Rocco. "I wanna see who won! Even though I think we can all agree that *I'm* the ultimate winner here. My ads on both channels made me sell out of Nanner Noms TWICE already! I have a waitlist with twenty names on it!"

"Don't you mean *our* ads?" Rue chimed in while filing her claws. "They wouldn't have been so popular if it wasn't for our fierce Spirit Week costumes that I designed."

"Okay, let's hear it, Rocco," said Connie. "Which team has more views?"

PURR FECT 9 EMBRACE THE PURRFECT IN YOU!

Rocco cleared his throat importantly. "All right then, here goes! The *Octopup Adventures* vlog has a grand total of four hundred eighty-five views."

Connie and Keen cheered. Peachy and Gertie clapped to be good sports, but stopped quickly so Rocco could continue.

"And the *Be Pawsitive!* vlog has a total of . . . five hundred two views! Congrats, Peachy and Gertie! You groovy gals are the winners!"

Peachy and Gertie were shocked. Had their videos really beaten out Connie and Keen's crazy stunts?

"Wow," said Connie, clearly disappointed. "Well, congratulations. It was a close race, but you won fair and square!"

"So you two get to host the *Purrfect9* vlog from now on!" Keen said cheerfully. "You both deserve it!"

Peachy and Gertie high-fived, finally letting it sink in that they had won. "Gertie, you were right all along!" Peachy said, beaming. "We didn't need something wild and flashy to get attention. We just have to be ourselves and try to help our school."

Gertie grinned back. "Yeah! But . . . you know what? Connie's right, too. It was a really close race. Their vlog was really popular, too." Gertie paused, clearly thinking very hard about something. "Peachy, who says the *Purrfect9* vlog has to be about only one thing?"

Peachy raised her eyebrows. "I guess it doesn't have to be," she admitted. "What are you saying?"

"I'm saying, what if you and I keep hosting our advice vlog—but in some videos, Connie and Keen can join in, too, and do their own funny segments? I think everyone who reads or watches *Purrfect9* will like both."

"Yeah!" Keen said. "We can call it 'Connie and Keen's Crash Zone!'"

"Cool!" said Connie. "I'm in."

CONNIE & KEEN'S
CRASH ZONE!

Peachy smiled. "That's a great idea, Gertie. I'm in, too! We can announce the news about the new vlog in our live video at the pup rally."

"And," said Connie. "I think I have an idea for our first Crash Zone stunt . . ."

"Helloooooo, Happy Tails!" Gary the Gorilla shouted to the cheering students in the stands. Gary was always the announcer for Happy Tails pup rallies because he didn't even need a megaphone to be loud enough for the entire gymnasium to hear him.

"It's been a great Spirit Week this year," Gary said. "You all really showed your Happy Tails spirit, as seen by the awesome photos Rue took of your costumes each day for *Purrfect9*." Gary nodded to Rue sitting in the stands.

GO TIGERS!

"And during the big game tonight, we're going to CRUSH THE PAWCADEMY PIRATES ONCE AND FOR ALL!" Gary bellowed over the cheers. "But first," he said, more calmly. "Before that, and before a performance from our two-time championship-winning pup squad—Peachy and Gertie from *Purrfect9* will film a special video."

"Thanks, Gary," said Gertie as she and Peachy took the stage. Rocco was filming them from the stands— and weirdly, Gertie was holding two giant cream pies. "We wanted to make a special announcement. Thanks to all of you for watching our vlogs this week! We had no idea both of them would be so popular. So, we're going to combine them into one brand-new super vlog!"

"You can still write to *Be Pawsitive!* for advice," Peachy said. "But we'll also feature extra, super-funny special segments with Connie and Keen—like right now!"

On cue, Connie and Keen joined Peachy and Gertie. Gertie handed the pies she was holding to Keen, and Connie took the microphone. "Some of you may know that I was the one who convinced Keen to share that video of him wiping out and getting hit with the Frisbee," she said. "He didn't want to do it, but I convinced him that everyone would love it. Which, well, you did." The audience laughed. "But still, what's fair is fair . . ."

Keen jumped in. "Connie agreed to let me get a little harmless payback on camera," he said with a mischievous smile. "Since I agreed to share a goofy video of myself for the vlog, so did she." With that, he tossed the giant cream pies right into Connie's face.

And that was the video that got the most views of all.

I Only Have Pies for You!

1,231 views

A frightful time later . . .

HAPPY TAILS

SPOOKTACULAR!

CAN YOU SURVIVE THE HAUNTED HALLS?

IT'S FINALLY MY TIME TO SHINE!

Boo!

To continued .